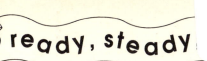

ready, steady

Cyril's Cats:
Mouse Practice

Written and
illustrated by Shoo Rayner

Puffin Books

for
Jessie

PUFFIN BOOKS

Published by the Penguin Group
Penguin Books Ltd, 27 Wrights Lane, London W8 5TZ, England
Penguin Books USA Inc., 375 Hudson Street, New York, New York 10014, USA
Penguin Books Australia Ltd, Ringwood, Victoria, Australia
Penguin Books Canada Ltd, 10 Alcorn Avenue, Toronto, Ontario, Canada M4V 3B2
Penguin Books (NZ) Ltd, 182–190 Wairau Road, Auckland 10, New Zealand

Penguin Books Ltd, Registered Offices: Harmondsworth, Middlesex, England

First published in Puffin Books 1996
10 9 8 7 6 5 4 3 2 1

Text and illustrations copyright © Shoo Rayner, 1996
All rights reserved

The moral right of the author/illustrator has been asserted

Filmset in Monotype Bembo Schoolbook

Printed in England by Clays Ltd, St Ives plc

CONTENTS

A CHIP OFF THE OLD BLOCK

Cyril had the biggest surprise of his life when his cat Charlie had four dear little kittens. Cyril had always thought that Charlie was a boy!

At first he wondered if he should change Charlie's name to Charlotte or Charlene, but in the end he decided to carry on calling her Charlie. After all, they were both a little bit old to start changing their ways.

Every day Cyril watched the kittens grow bigger and stronger. They often made him laugh. They played hide and seek, and they played rough and tumble.

They
tried to
climb the
curtains,
but fell off.

They found sticky places where
they got stuck.

They found some very funny
things to sleep in.

Cyril had to be careful where he sat down! The kittens grew bigger and bigger. "You lot are going to eat me out of house and home," he said one day.

I'm afraid we'll have to find new homes for you all

The two stripy kittens went to live with Cyril's granddaughters, Kate and Sally. They had always wanted a cat. When Charlie had kittens, they pestered their mum night and day until she gave in and let them have one each.

They called their kittens Tilly and Tabitha.

Mrs Taylor, who lived next door to Cyril, had noticed that one of the kittens looked just like her cat Hercules.

"I don't suppose you'd like him, would you?" Cyril asked hopefully.

Mrs Taylor said she would love to have him. "He really does look like Hercules. Anyone would think that they were related! I think I'll call him Hector."

11

Only the little grey kitten was left, but Cyril couldn't think of anyone who would want him. He picked the kitten up and looked at him closely.

"My, you're a chip off the old block, aren't you? You look just like Charlie did when she was a kitten."

Without the other kittens being there, Cyril got to know the little grey kitten quite well. Over the next few days he often found himself saying, "You really are a chip off the old block." And it was true, he looked and behaved just like Charlie had as a kitten.

Charlie watched Cyril cut a piece
of card out of a cereal packet and
carefully write out a notice.

Grey Kitten
Caring home
wanted for a
small grey kitten
very friendly
Phone 237
Cyril 5

"I'm just going to the shop,
Charlie. I'll put this advert in their
window. Someone is bound to
want a little grey kitten."

Cyril told the shopkeeper that the kitten would grow up to be a wonderful cat, because Charlie was so friendly and the kitten was just like her. The shopkeeper put Cyril's card into the window for everyone to see.

It wasn't long before someone phoned and asked if they could come and see the kitten.

"No problem," said Cyril, "you can come round now if you like."

Charlie had other ideas. She'd already lost three kittens and didn't want to lose another.

As the doorbell rang, she grabbed
the kitten by the scruff of his neck
and dragged him through the cat-
flap,

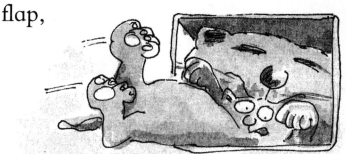

down the garden path,

and under
the shed.

"Now, stay there. Don't move and
don't make a sound until I say
so," Charlie said firmly.

21

When Charlie came back through
the cat-flap she found Cyril talking
to a woman and her two sons.

"This is the kitten's mother," said
Cyril. "The kitten is a real chip off
the old block. He looks just like
Charlie did when she was little.
But I can't think where he's got to.
He was here a minute ago."

Cyril called all over the house, "Here, Kitty, Kitty!" They all went out into the garden, but no kitten was to be found. As the search went on, Charlie pretended to look worried.

Cyril told the woman that he
would phone her when the kitten
had been found, then he carried
on searching in cupboards and
looking under beds.

Charlie pretended to be very upset. Even though she was hungry, she didn't eat her food. She sat in her cat basket and looked sad.

When Cyril had checked every
last place at least three times, he
sat down and looked at Charlie.
Charlie looked up at him. Her
face was as sad as it could be.

They stayed like that for at least
five minutes, while Cyril had a
good think.

Cyril sighed deeply. "Oh, Charlie, I hope that little kitten is all right. I do miss him so. I don't think I could let him live anywhere else now. This place wouldn't be the same without him."

That was just what Charlie wanted to hear. She sloped off through the cat-flap still pretending to look sad. Then she dragged the kitten back through the cat-flap, wearing a huge smile on her face, and dropped him in front of Cyril.

"Oh, Charlie!" he exclaimed.
"You clever old thing, you found
him." Cyril lifted up the kitten to
see if he was all right. "My, you
really are a chip off the old block,
aren't you? In fact I think that's
what I should call you: Chip!"

Cyril sorted out the cats' bed. He freshened up their food and gave them some milk to drink and then waited until they had both settled down.

"Right then," he whispered, "I'd better go and phone that lady to tell her that I've decided to keep you after all . . . Welcome home, Chip."

Charlie smiled and Chip snuggled up close to her. Before long the two cats were purring happily.

MOUSE PRACTICE

One bright, sunny morning
Charlie and Chip woke up. They
yawned and stretched and washed
themselves clean.

Chip was still only a kitten so
Charlie helped by licking Chip's
ears and all those other important
places that he couldn't quite reach.

When they had finished, Chip climbed into the litter tray to finish off his morning routine.

Cyril came down to make himself a cup of tea. He looked in the litter tray.

"Pooh!" he said, wrinkling up his nose. "I think it's time Chip started house-training. Charlie, you'd better show him how things are done around here."

Cyril carefully emptied the litter
tray into a plastic bag, which he
tied up and put outside in the
dustbin. Then he washed his hands,
made his tea and gave the cats
their breakfast.

"Come on, eat up. We've got a lot to do today," said Charlie. "I'll teach you to use the cat-flap first."

So, when the bowls were clean,
Charlie showed Chip how the flap
worked. She went out . . . and
came in again.

"See?" she said. "It's easy. Just
push with your head and through
you go."

Of course it wasn't so easy for
Chip. He had to jump up a bit
and then he got stuck in the
middle. Charlie had to shove him
through the rest of the way.

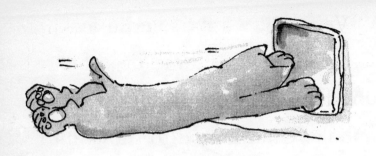

After a few practice goes, Chip
worked out that he could sort of
run at the flap, with his head
down and his eyes closed, and sort
of tumble through the hole, and
sort of land on all fours on the
other side.

"Well done," said Charlie, licking a dirty patch on Chip's neck that she hadn't noticed before.

She took Chip to a quiet part of the garden where Cyril had been digging the day before.

Charlie said in a teaching voice:
"Now that you can get out
through the flap you won't need
your litter tray any more. This is
where you'll come in the
mornings."

She showed him how to dig a little hole and then how to fill it up again so Cyril wouldn't notice.

Charlie took Chip to the old lilac tree at the bottom of the garden. There she showed him how to scratch his claws and keep them nice and sharp. And all the while she told him about being a cat.

"Cats catch mice, that's our job. You must always be on guard, ready to pounce at a moment's notice. You'll need a lot of practice, so you can start by trying to catch my tail."

Chip crouched down and watched his mother's tail sway from side to side. He made ready to pounce, but as he leaped through the air Charlie pulled her tail away and the poor kitten landed in a clump of daisies.

They practised all morning.
Sometimes Charlie would let Chip
catch her tail so that he wouldn't
get bored, but his claws were
sharp, so she didn't let him win
very often!

They grew tired of the game and
looked for a quiet place to rest.
Charlie told Chip how to hunt
mice and how she had once scared
off a rat that had never come back.

Chip thought for a while, then he asked, "Mum, if our job is to catch mice then why haven't we seen any yet?"

Charlie smiled. "I caught them all!
Don't worry, there'll be lots more
for you to catch. Always be on the
look-out; even when you are
asleep you must listen out for
them."

Cyril was whistling and digging in the vegetable garden and Mrs Taylor was clipping her roses next door. The two cats grew more and more drowsy until they were both sprawled out, fast asleep in the warm sunshine.

Charlie and Chip woke with a start. The look on his mother's face told Chip that something exciting was about to happen.

"There's something on the other side of the fence," Charlie whispered. "It might be a mouse. If it comes through that gap, jump on it."

Chip could hear the noise. His heart thumped as he waited to see his first mouse.

All was quiet. Cyril stopped
digging. Mrs Taylor stopped
clipping. Chip waited . . . and
waited . . . and waited.

Suddenly a flash of black and white fur shot through the gap. Without a second thought, Chip pounced. He grabbed hold of the mouse and the mouse grabbed hold of him. Together they rolled and tumbled across the flower-beds.

Chip was surprised that the mouse was so strong. He was just about to give up the fight when he heard someone laughing. He and the mouse stopped to see what was so funny.

Cyril was shaking with laughter and Mrs Taylor, who had been watching from over the fence, laughed too. In the flower-bed Charlie and Hercules, the cat who lived next door, were smiling.

Chip looked at the mouse and the mouse looked at him. But it wasn't a mouse, it was Hector, his brother who lived next door!

"I thought you were a mouse!"
said Hector.

"I thought you were a mouse,
too!" said Chip.

Cyril had watched the whole
performance. He picked Charlie
up and hugged her.

"Oh, Charlie, that kitten really is a chip off the old block. One day he'll be as good a mouser as you are, but you'll always be *my* Charlie."

Cyril tickled Charlie behind the ears, then he went back to his digging. Mrs Taylor went back to clipping her rose bushes, leaving Charlie and Hercules to watch the kittens play the afternoon away.

63

ready, steady, read!